What Is Sight?

Jennifer Boothroyd

Lerner Publications Company
Minneapolis

For my grandparents, Donald and Mary

Lerner Publications Company
A division of Lerner Publishing Group, Inc.
241 First Avenue North
Minneapolis, MN 55401 U.S.A.

Website address: www.lernerbooks.com

Library of Congress Cataloging-in-Publication Data

Boothroyd, Jennifer, 1972–
        What is sight? / by Jennifer Boothroyd.
            p.   cm. — (Lightning bolt books™—Your amazing senses)
        Includes index.
    ISBN 978–0–7613–4248–9 (lib. bdg. : alk. paper)
        1. Vision—Juvenile literature. I. Title.
    QP475.7.B66 2010
    612.8´4—dc22   2008051849

Manufactured in the United States of America
1 2 3 4 5 6 — BP — 15 14 13 12 11 10

Contents

Gathering Information

Look at the clothes you are wearing.

What color are they? Is there a pattern or a picture on them?

This girl's skirt has a colorful plaid pattern.

5

You are
seeing what
your clothes
look like.

Seeing is one of your five senses. You use your eyes to see things.

Eyes help you see to read, color pictures, do homework, and play.

Your sense of sight helps you learn about the world. It can also protect you from danger.

Thanks to your sense of sight, you can take in information and explore your surroundings.

Your Eyes

How do your eyes help you see? When you see something, your eyes let in light through the pupils. The pupils are the dark circles in the center of your eyes.

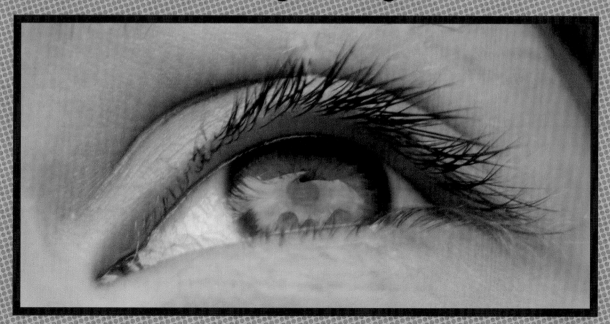

Then the light moves through the curved part of your eyes called the lens.

The lens turns the light into a picture on the back of your eyes. The picture is upside down. But your brain flips the picture over.

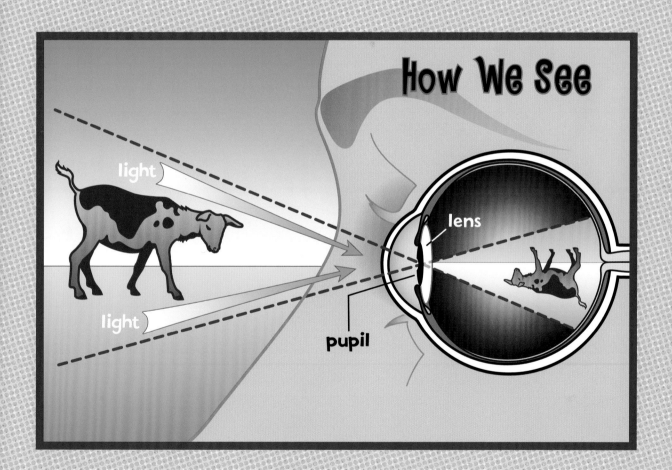

Your eyes help you see both this boy and his reflection in the car window.

Then your brain tells you what you are seeing!

Colors

Your eyes let you see many different colors.

How many colors do you see in this painting?

You can see a green frog.

You can see an orange Popsicle.

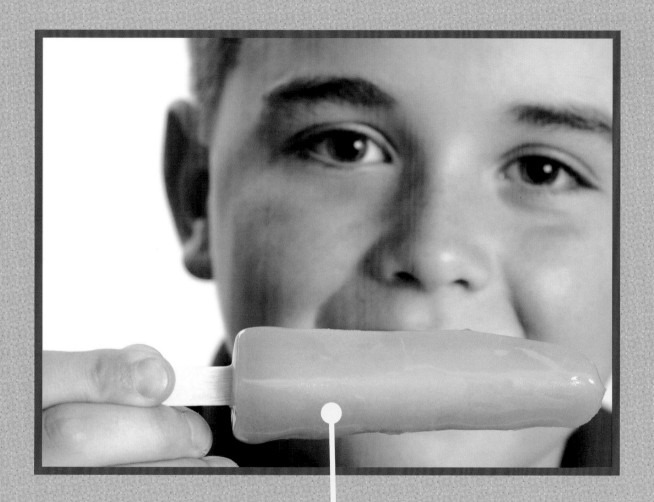

The world is full of beautiful colors—and your eyes let you see them all.

Your eyes need light to see different colors.

Without light, you couldn't see these colorful candies.

It is hard
to tell
what color
your socks
are in the
dark!

17

Protection from Danger

Seeing can protect you from danger. You can see when it is safe to cross the street.

Reading signs and watching traffic keep you safe.

You can see the exit
sign to lead the way
out in an emergency.

Distance

Your eyes can see things at different distances.

They can see words in a book
that you are holding.

You need good
close-up vision
to read.

They can see leaves on a tree in your neighbor's yard.

You need good long-distance vision to see trees that are far away.

23

Some people have trouble seeing things that are far away. They look blurry.

A vision problem called nearsightedness can make faraway objects—like this sign—look blurry.

Things up close might look fuzzy to others.

A vision problem called farsightedness can make it hard to see close-up objects.

Glasses can help people who have trouble seeing. Glasses help the eyes focus.

Seeing is an important sense. You use it every day.

This boy is using his sense of sight—as well as his sense of touch—as he plays in a stream.

Activity
Test Your Depth Perception

Depth perception is the ability to judge how far away objects are from one another. Your eyes must work together for you to have good depth perception. Want to see how depth perception works? Ask an adult if you can try this experiment to test your depth perception.

What you need:
Two cotton swabs

What you do:

Hold a cotton swab horizontally in each hand. Hold your arms straight out in front of you. Close one eye. (If you can't hold one eye closed, you can ask a friend to gently hold his or her hand over your eye.) Slowly move your hands toward each other and try to touch the ends of the cotton swabs together. If you miss, keep trying. Then open both eyes and try again.

It is easier to touch the cotton swabs together when you use both of your eyes. That's because your eyes work together to let you see the cotton swabs from different angles. Your brain uses the information that it gets from your eyes to help you judge the distance between the cotton swabs.

Glossary

blurry: unclear or hard to see

depth perception: the ability to judge how far away objects are from one another

glasses: glass or plastic lenses set in frames. People wear glasses to help their eyes focus.

lens: the curved part of your eye that lets you focus

pupil: the dark circle in the center of your eye. Your eye lets in light through its pupil.

sense: one of the powers that people and animals use to learn about their surroundings. The five senses are sight, hearing, touch, taste, and smell.

Further Reading

Haddon, Jean. *Make Sense!* Minneapolis: Millbrook Press, 2007.

Hewitt, Sally. *Look Here!* New York: Crabtree Publishing Company, 2008.

Kids Health: How the Body Works
http://kidshealth.org/kid/htbw

Nelson, Robin. *Seeing and Hearing Well.* Minneapolis: Lerner Publications Company, 2006.

Rotner, Shelley. *Senses in the City.* Minneapolis: Millbrook Press, 2008.

Index

Photo Acknowledgments

The images in this book are used with the permission of: © Tatiana Popova/istockphoto.com, p. 1; © Scott Barrow, Inc./SuperStock, p. 2; © Chris Ladd/Taxi/Getty Images, p. 4; © Julie Caruso/Independent Picture Service, p. 5; © Jamie Grill/Iconica/Getty Images, p. 6; © Gallo Images-Anthony Strack/Gallo images ROOTS RF collection/Getty Images, pp. 7, 22; © Stephan K. Hall/SuperStock, p. 8; © Julie Caruso, p. 9; © Juan Silva/Stone/Getty Images, p. 10; © Laura Westlund/Independent Picture Service, p. 11; © Kohei Hara/Getty Images, p. 12; © age fotostock/SuperStock, p. 13; © Digital Vision/Getty Images, p. 14; © iStockphoto.com/Fertnig, p. 15; © Icefields/Dreamstime.com, p. 16; © David Roth/Photodisc/Getty Images, p. 17; © Photononstop/SuperStock, p. 18; © Jenny Boothroyd, p. 19; © Todd Strand/Independent Picture Service, pp. 20, 24; © David Deas/DK Stock/Getty Images, p. 21; © Gary John Norman/The Image Bank/Getty Images, p. 23; © BLOOMimage/Getty Images, p. 25; © Peter Dazeley/Photographer's Choice RR/Getty Images, p. 26; © iStockphoto.com/asiseeit, p. 27; © iStockphoto.com/StuartDuncanSmith, p. 28; © Kohei Hara/Digital Vision/Getty Images, p. 30; © Zeid/eStock Photo/Alamy, p. 31.

Front cover: © Dwight Eschliman/Stone/Getty Images.

LAND SHAPES

MOUNTAIN

Author
Brian Knapp, BSc, PhD
Art Director
Duncan McCrae, BSc
Editor
Rita Owen
Illustrator
David Hardy
Print consultants
Landmark Production Consultants Ltd
Printed and bound in Hong Kong
Produced by
EARTHSCAPE EDITIONS

First published in the USA in 1993 by
GROLIER EDUCATIONAL CORPORATION,
Sherman Turnpike, Danbury, CT 06816

Copyright © 1992
Atlantic Europe Publishing Company Limited

Library of Congress #92–072045

Cataloging information may be obtained
directly from Grolier Educational Corporation

Title ISBN   0–7172–7177–3

Set ISBN   0–7172–7176–5

Acknowledgements. The publishers would like to
thank the following: Leighton Park School, Martin
Morris and Redlands County Primary School.

Picture credits. All photographs from the
Earthscape Editions photographic library except
the following (t=top, b=bottom, l=left, r=right):
David Higgs 25; United States Geological Survey
13b; ZEFA 8/9, 17t, 18/19, 19t, 29t, 34/35.
Cover picture: Half Dome, Yosemite, California, USA.

In this book you will find some words that have been shown in **bold** type. There is a full explanation of each of these words on page 36.

On many pages you will find experiments that you might like to try for yourself. They have been put in a blue box like this.

In this book mi means miles, y means yards and ft means feet.

These people appear on a number of pages to help you to know the size of some landshapes.

CONTENTS

Introduction

This is a book about mountains – massive peaks and ridges of rock that rise clear of their surroundings. Mountains are among the world's biggest and most spectacular landshapes and they can be found in all parts of the world; from the equator to the poles and from the middle of the oceans to the centers of continents.

Some mountains stand on their own, like giant cones. These have been built by **volcanos** and many still **erupt**. Other mountains occur in long narrow bands with many peaks separated by deep valleys. These are called **mountain ranges** and they are formed when parts of the Earth's surface rocks push against each other. Usually, mountain ranges occur side by side in groups that make up **mountain chains**.

As mountains build higher, so the peaks and ridges are attacked by biting frosts and deep valleys are carved by glaciers and fast-flowing rivers.

In this book you can find out about the way mountains are formed and how each shape tells its own story. Enjoy exploring the landshapes of mountains by turning to any page you choose.

Take care in the mountains

Mountains are some of the world's most exciting landshapes and you are sure to want to visit them. But never go up mountains without the correct clothing and footwear and without a qualified and experienced mountain leader. Mountains can be dangerous places for the unwary and deaths have occurred because people have gone walking unprepared.

Chapter 1
How mountains are built

What makes mountains?

Mountains are like a vast jigsaw – shaped into many kinds of patterns, built up of many kinds of rocks and worn away by frost, ice and water.

Many different types of rock can be found squeezed together. Each rock stands up to frost, ice and water in its own special way. This is why no two mountains look the same.

Rocks from below the seas
Many mountain rocks are 'second-hand' – they are made with the **eroded** waste of old mountains that have been carried by rivers and settled down at the bottoms of ancient seas. These are called sedimentary rocks, an example being sandstone.

This is a valley within a mountain chain. It was shaped first by rivers (see page 30), then by glaciers (see page 26), and since the glaciers have melted away it is being eroded by rivers again.

This is gneiss. The wavy lines were formed when the rocks were squeezed into bands. This is a very tough rock.

This is sandstone, a rock made from an ancient beach.

Rocks from pressure
As rocks are squashed together to make mountains, some rocks begin to melt and change their properties. They are called metamorphic rocks, examples being gneiss and slate.

10

Any part of a mountain that stands up sharply above its surroundings is called a peak. Most peaks are made sharper by the effects of frost (see page 24).

A ridge separates two valleys. Many ridges in mountain areas are knife-edged (see page 28).

This rock is called granite. The crystals were formed when it was molten.

Rocks from inside the Earth
As mountains form, molten material flows up from deep inside the Earth. This cools into igneous rocks such as granite.

Why mountains grow

The surface of the Earth is made up of an outer layer of rocks called the **crust**. The crust is not a single unbroken layer, but rather it consists of many giant pieces, called **plates**. All the plates move slowly across the Earth.

Nearly all of the Earth's mountains are made at the edges of these plates. Sometimes the plates push against each other and crumple the edges. These produce ranges of **fold mountains**.

In other places the edges of plates pull apart, cracking the crust and moving blocks of rock up and down. This causes **block mountains** to form.

If one plate slides under the other, molten rock flows up from within the Earth and the mountains are volcanos.

Plates

The picture on the right shows the most important cracks in the Earth's crust and the main plates. Mountains are being built at all these plate edges, and sometimes mountains form beneath the ocean surface.

The plate shapes change from time to time. Old mountains now far from the present plate edges show where the edges were millions of years ago.

This plate contains the continent of South America and part of the Atlantic Ocean floor.

The Andes form at this boundary

Imagine a hard-boiled egg blown up to be as big as the Earth. The brittle shell now makes the Earth's surface rocks, or crust.

Below the crust the Earth is soft and made of hot molten rock.

Imagine tapping the egg with a spoon until the surface is cracked into large pieces. On the Earth these pieces of crust are the plates.

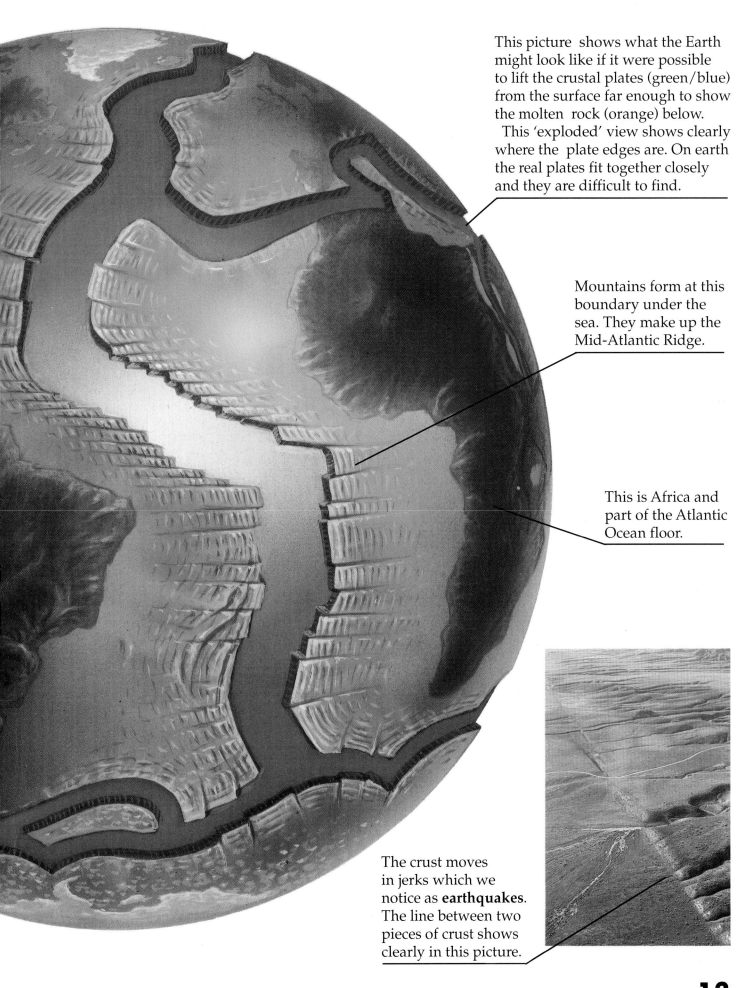

This picture shows what the Earth might look like if it were possible to lift the crustal plates (green/blue) from the surface far enough to show the molten rock (orange) below. This 'exploded' view shows clearly where the plate edges are. On earth the real plates fit together closely and they are difficult to find.

Mountains form at this boundary under the sea. They make up the Mid-Atlantic Ridge.

This is Africa and part of the Atlantic Ocean floor.

The crust moves in jerks which we notice as **earthquakes**. The line between two pieces of crust shows clearly in this picture.

Block mountains

These form where the Earth's crust bulges upwards and where it also begins to pull apart. As the land is pushed higher the crust cracks and some blocks fall back down, leaving other blocks as tall mountain ranges.

Basin and range

Block mountains are often dramatic. Long lines of mountains are separated by wide flat valleys or basins. The coastal Flinders Range near Adelaide in South Australia is a good example of mountain blocks.

This picture shows part of the block mountains of south-west USA, an area known as 'Basin and Range' country.

There is a sharp boundary between the mountain block and the valley block. It is called a **fault** line.

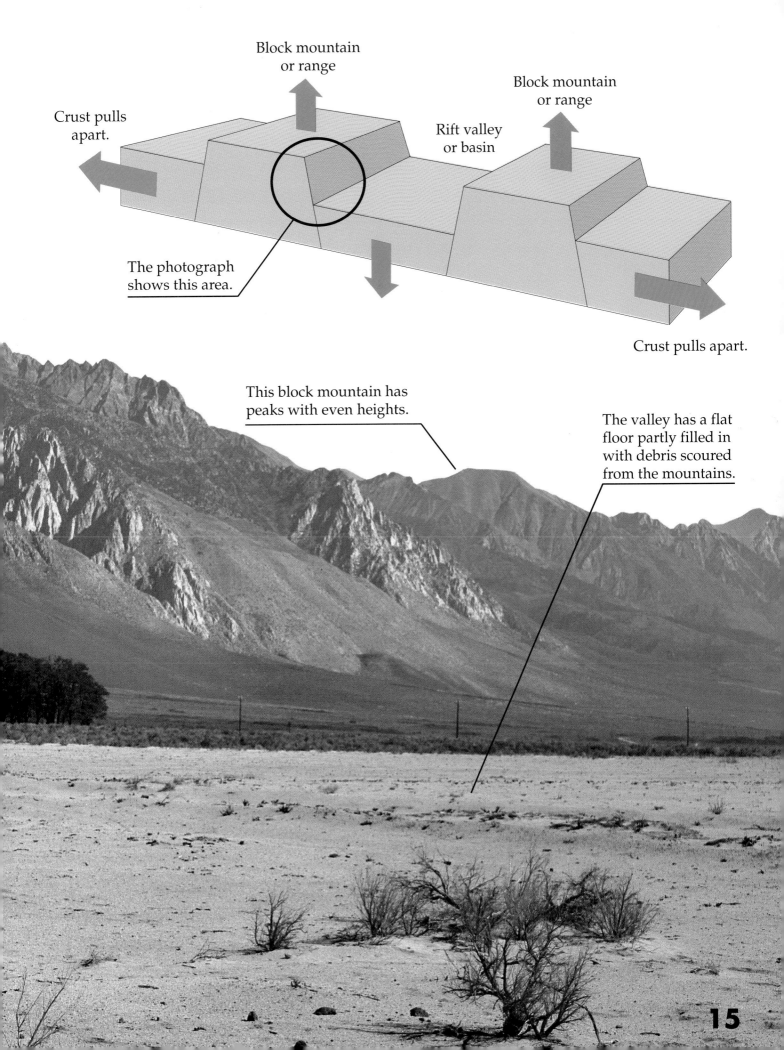

Crust pulls apart.

Block mountain
or range

Block mountain
or range

Rift valley
or basin

The photograph
shows this area.

Crust pulls apart.

This block mountain has
peaks with even heights.

The valley has a flat
floor partly filled in
with debris scoured
from the mountains.

15

Volcanic mountains

Not all mountains are made of folded rocks. Many are the result of volcanic eruptions.

The shape of the volcano depends on the type of **lava** and ash that erupts from the volcano. Some eruptions produce very runny lava, creating volcanos that are very broad, but with gentle sides such as those of the Hawaiian islands.

At the other extreme are the volcanos that erupt with great explosions. These throw out ash and cinders that quickly build into a steep-sided mountain like Mt. St. Helens in the north-west United States.

This piece of rock was once molten and flowed from a volcano like the one shown on the facing page. Notice the small bubbles inside the lava. They were formed from gas trapped within the lava before it cooled.

This is Mt. Adams, one of many volcanos that make up the western Cascade Range in North America. The volcano has erupted mainly from its center, building up a large cone. But it has also erupted in other places, giving rise, for example, to the smaller cone that makes the 'shoulder' on the right.

For more information on volcanos see the book Volcano *in the Landshapes set.*

A volcanic mountain in the making
Volcanos erupt through natural pipes in the Earth's crust which lead up from chambers containing huge volumes of molten lava deep below the surface.

During an eruption molten rock (lava) reaches the surface quickly, sometimes making an explosion and sending clouds of ash high into the sky.
  This volcano shown in this picture is producing a fountain of lava which acts as the source for rivers of lava which then flow down the flanks.

As the lava cools it turns from red to black. Many of the recently cooled lava trails can be seen in this picture as ropy-looking black lines.

As lava flows build on each other they gradually form the cone of the volcanic mountain. Many volcanos are a mixture of deposits of ash and lava.

Island chains

Some volcanos erupt in the oceans and make islands. Usually the islands form into long strings, showing that there is a crack between the Earth's crustal plates.

Islands are especially common in the Pacific Ocean. Some of the more famous groups are Japan, Hawaii, Indonesia and Papua New Guinea. A famous volcanic island in the North Atlantic Ocean is Iceland.

Hawaii, undersea giants

The Hawaiian islands are a string of ocean mountains that stretch across the Pacific Ocean for over 600 mi.

They have an unusual history. Imagine the sea bed as a carpet that is continually being dragged in one direction. Under the carpet is a red-hot rock. If the carpet is thin, or if the movement slows for a moment, the hot rock will burn a hole through the carpet. After a while there will be a line of holes, each formed one after another.

The Hawaiian islands have formed over a 'hot spot' of molten lava beneath the ocean floor. When it gets the chance, the molten rock bursts through the crust and makes a new volcano. Mauna Loa is the world's biggest individual mountain and is still an active volcano.

The volcanic island of Oahu, Hawaii rises out of the Pacific Ocean. Its sides have been eroded into valleys by rivers. Many volcanos yield fertile soils which allow plants to grow easily, even on the flanks of an active volcano.

Many islands make up the region known as Polynesia in the Pacific Ocean. In each case the tip of a volcano forms the core of the island. In this picture a ring of coral (the white band with the runway) has formed a reef which encircles the island.

To imagine the real size of the island mountain, think of the mountain sides going down to the ocean bed thousands of yards below.

*For more information on coral islands
see the book* Reef *in the Landshapes set.*

Fold mountains

Fold mountains make up the world's biggest mountain systems. Often range after range of folded rocks stretch right across a continent.

Fold mountains form when, over tens of millions of years, two parts of the Earth's crust push together.

Eventually even the strongest rocks cannot stand up to such pressure and so they begin to bend and crack, while at the same time molten rock squeezes into the mountain core.

Wherever you see rocks that have been curved, or folded, you know that enormous forces must have acted in the past. Sometimes the folds are easy to see, such as in sea cliffs. At other times the folds are much bigger and make up whole mountain ranges (see pages 32-35).

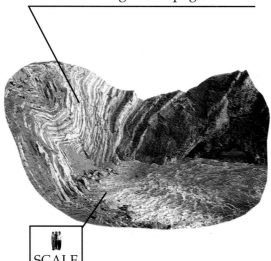

SCALE

Erosion by ice has exposed the folded rocks that make up this mountain. If you look carefully you will see that the rocks of the peak are folded into a saucer-shape.

Find out about fold mountains

Many of the effects of plates moving together can be demonstrated by simple activities that you can try.

If you push a table cover over a table it will crease up into folds in patterns broadly similar to those that form on the Earth. Try pushing the cover in different ways to see how many patterns of fold mountains you can produce.

Modelling clay can also be used. When used as sheets it will produce quite realistic effects. If the modelling clay is cold it will be slightly hard and so will crack as it folds, in the same way as rocks.

Always try to make realistic models. Use an atlas to find the shapes of mountain ranges. This is how the fold mountains on pages 33 and 35 were produced.

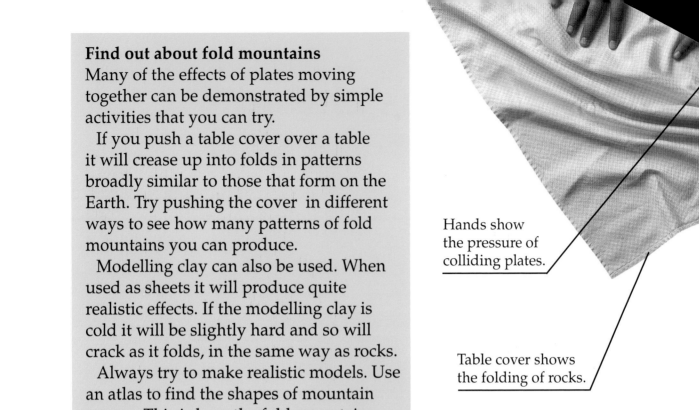

Hands show the pressure of colliding plates.

Table cover shows the folding of rocks.

Folding demonstrated by modelling clay.

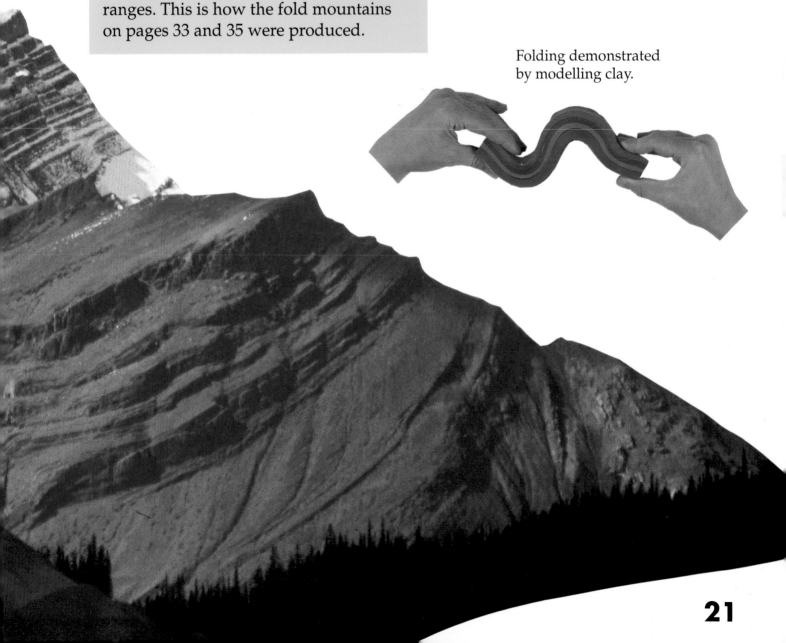

21

ow mountains change

Mountain cycle

Mountains become grand not just because the land is lifted up high, but also because of the cutting away, or erosion, by rivers, frost and ice.

  Without this natural 'sculpturing' the mountains would look a lot less interesting.

These glaciers in Greenland are sculpting new mountains as they cut into a tableland.

1. Rising

The first stage in the mountain cycle happens when the land is lifted up as plates collide. Sometimes volcanos make grand mountains directly, but more often the rocks are pushed up into a broad area of high land. Without the effects of water, frost and ice acting on the rock, it would remain a high featureless area called a tableland.

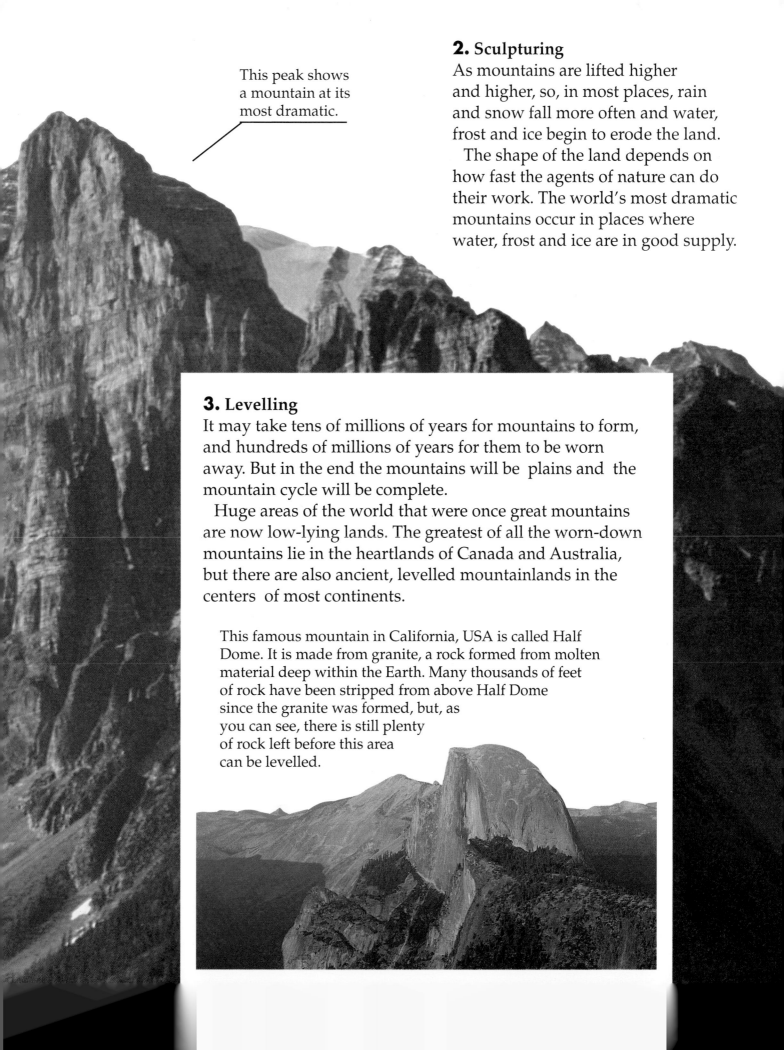

This peak shows a mountain at its most dramatic.

2. Sculpturing

As mountains are lifted higher and higher, so, in most places, rain and snow fall more often and water, frost and ice begin to erode the land.

The shape of the land depends on how fast the agents of nature can do their work. The world's most dramatic mountains occur in places where water, frost and ice are in good supply.

3. Levelling

It may take tens of millions of years for mountains to form, and hundreds of millions of years for them to be worn away. But in the end the mountains will be plains and the mountain cycle will be complete.

Huge areas of the world that were once great mountains are now low-lying lands. The greatest of all the worn-down mountains lie in the heartlands of Canada and Australia, but there are also ancient, levelled mountainlands in the centers of most continents.

This famous mountain in California, USA is called Half Dome. It is made from granite, a rock formed from molten material deep within the Earth. Many thousands of feet of rock have been stripped from above Half Dome since the granite was formed, but, as you can see, there is still plenty of rock left before this area can be levelled.

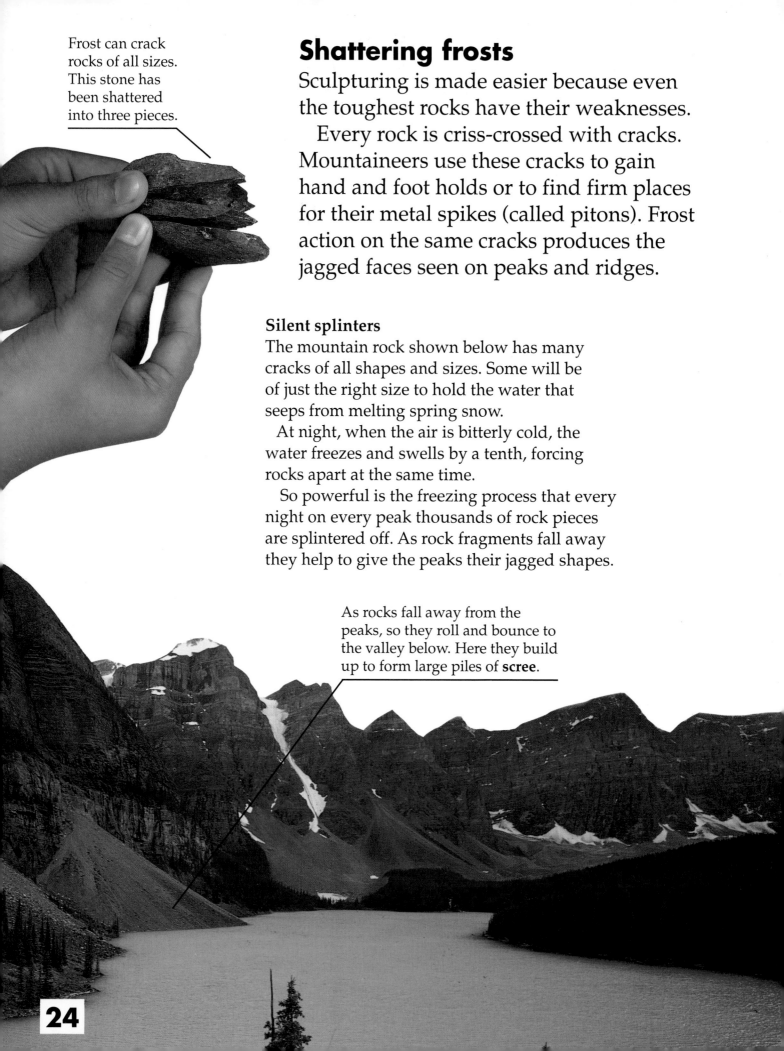

Frost can crack rocks of all sizes. This stone has been shattered into three pieces.

Shattering frosts

Sculpturing is made easier because even the toughest rocks have their weaknesses.

Every rock is criss-crossed with cracks. Mountaineers use these cracks to gain hand and foot holds or to find firm places for their metal spikes (called pitons). Frost action on the same cracks produces the jagged faces seen on peaks and ridges.

Silent splinters

The mountain rock shown below has many cracks of all shapes and sizes. Some will be of just the right size to hold the water that seeps from melting spring snow.

At night, when the air is bitterly cold, the water freezes and swells by a tenth, forcing rocks apart at the same time.

So powerful is the freezing process that every night on every peak thousands of rock pieces are splintered off. As rock fragments fall away they help to give the peaks their jagged shapes.

As rocks fall away from the peaks, so they roll and bounce to the valley below. Here they build up to form large piles of **scree**.

The cause of cracks
Rocks are formed deep below the ground surface where there are great pressures and no cracks in the rock.

As rivers and glaciers strip away the covering layers, so the buried rocks come closer to the surface. Because the pressure is less great they begin to crack. When exposed on the surface, the cracks are opened further by frost action.

The rock flake that provides a natural hand-hold for this mountaineer, has been opened up by frost. Eventually it will be forced from the mountain and fall to the valley to build a scree.

Gouging ice

In high mountains snow drifts build quickly. As the layers of snow get thicker, the deepest snow is sometimes squashed into ice.

When the weight of snow and ice is great enough, the ice is squeezed from mountain hollows or icefields and it moves down through valleys as glaciers, much like toothpaste is squeezed from a tube. These glaciers pick up small pieces of rock that have been loosened by frost and use them to gouge deeply into the mountain landscape.

Snow in a hollow readily builds thick enough to form ice.

This glacier is scouring the valley using trapped rocks. By eroding only on its bottom, a glacier deepens its valley and makes it U-shaped.

An icefield formed between mountain peaks. This is the source of large glaciers.

Ice is compact and heavy. It slides out of a hollow under its own weight.

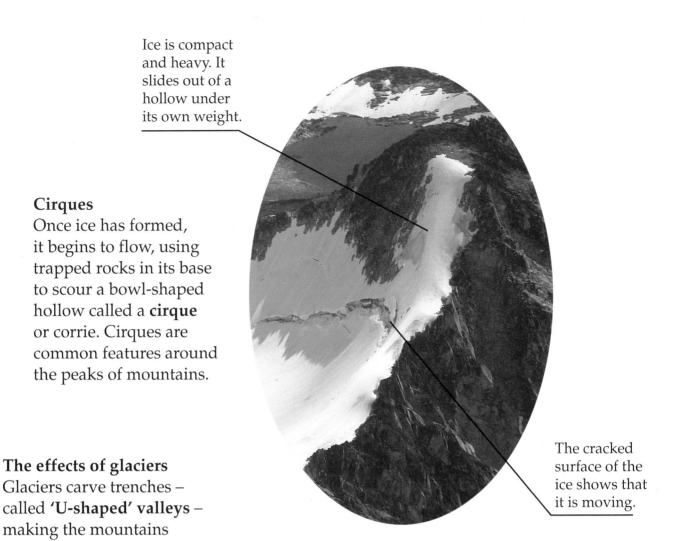

Cirques
Once ice has formed, it begins to flow, using trapped rocks in its base to scour a bowl-shaped hollow called a **cirque** or corrie. Cirques are common features around the peaks of mountains.

The cracked surface of the ice shows that it is moving.

The effects of glaciers
Glaciers carve trenches – called **'U-shaped' valleys** – making the mountains appear even more dramatic, as the picture below shows.

Cirques

For more information on the work of glaciers see the book Glacier *in the Landshapes set.*

Peaks and ridges

Peaks and ridges stand out clearly in many mountain landscapes. They are all that is left of an area that was once broader and less rugged.

Peaks are under attack from many sides, while ridges are under attack from two valleys. Here is how they are formed.

Horns

If several cirque glaciers scour ever-deepening bowls into the flanks of a peak, the peak will become sharpened. Sharp-pointed mountains are called horns.

Ice forms in hollows and gouges out a deep basin. This helps to turn a mountain peak into a horn.

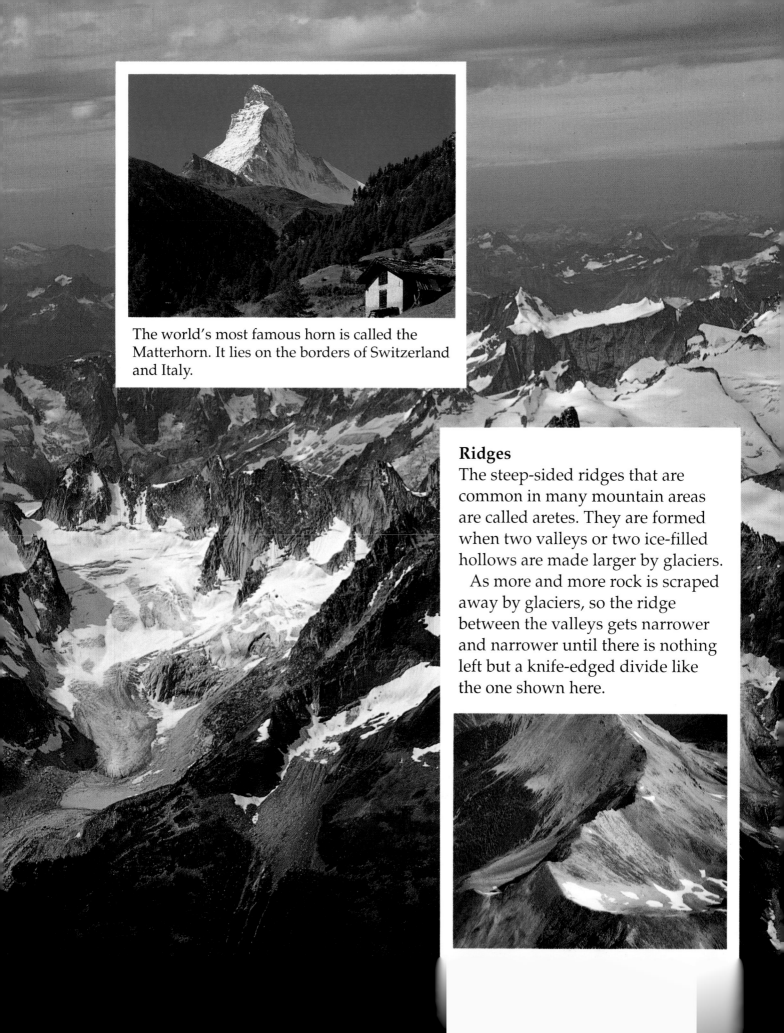

The world's most famous horn is called the Matterhorn. It lies on the borders of Switzerland and Italy.

Ridges

The steep-sided ridges that are common in many mountain areas are called aretes. They are formed when two valleys or two ice-filled hollows are made larger by glaciers.

As more and more rock is scraped away by glaciers, so the ridge between the valleys gets narrower and narrower until there is nothing left but a knife-edged divide like the one shown here.

Impatient rivers

As rivers flow swiftly from the mountains, they carry everything from the finest mud particles to great boulders. These are the tools that mountain rivers use to sculpture the land, widening valleys, making gorges, waterfalls, rapids and potholes.

Mountain slopes are often scored by numerous river valleys. In this picture you can see how headwater streams are eroding their way towards the summit of the mountain.

Boulder-strewn bed
A sure sign that rivers are plunging quickly down their courses is the presence of boulders across the bed.

Only fast-flowing rivers can carry boulders and, by bouncing them down valleys during times of rapid snowmelt or during storms, rivers rapidly deepen their valleys.

For more information about rivers see the book River *in the Landshapes set.*

Gorges

A gorge is a trench that has been cut so quickly by a river that the sides have had no time to widen into a valley. Gorges are common in mountains where rivers often pick out lines of weakness such as faults.

Because of the rapid rate of trenching, no soil forms on the sides of the gorge and they remain rocky and barren.

Chapter 4
Mountains of the world

The Rocky mountains

This mountain chain divides North America in two. The Rockies is still one of the greatest mountain chains in the world even though it is no longer at a plate boundary.

Some of the most spectacular Rockies' peaks are found in the Banff and Jasper National Parks of Canada. The picture on the right shows part of Jasper National Park near the Athabasca Glacier.

Mountain front
This picture shows how the Rocky Mountains rise like a giant wall in Grand Teton National Park, USA.

As rivers and glaciers carve the mountain landscape, so the debris is carried east to the lowlands, where it adds to the vast level area known as the Great Plains.

Mountain chain

The Rockies contain many ranges, or groups of mountain peaks. Each range tells of a differently folded band of rock. Between lie the plains made flat by debris dropped by the mountain rivers.

This table cover model shows the broad pattern of folded ranges in the Rocky Mountains made using the technique shown on page 21. To get accurate information on ranges you should refer to an atlas. The hands show the directions in which the pressures must have been applied for these mountains to form parallel ranges.

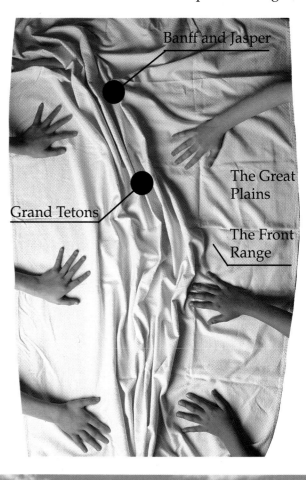

Banff and Jasper

The Great Plains

Grand Tetons

The Front Range

The summit of
Mount Everest

The Himalayas

In Sanskrit the word Himalaya means
him: snow; *alaya*: home. It is the world's
largest mountain chain and it contains
the world's largest land peaks.

The Himalayas are rising by about
6 cm a year and as the glaciers and
rivers continue to tear at the rocks,
the most spectacular mountain
landscape on Earth is being created.

Mt. Everest and the other high Himalayan peaks rise above the cloud level for much of the year.

Mt. Everest

This picture shows the view of the peak of Mt. Everest (29, 028 ft) from the south (Nepalese) side.

Mt. Everest is a broad peak that is only a little higher than its neighbours. The Tibetan name for Mt. Everest is Sagamartha, land of eternal snows, and the snow from each peak forms the start of a giant glacier.

The roof of the world

The Himalayas have been crushed into one of two arcs. Between them is a huge slab of level rock called the Tibetan Plateau.

The folding of the Himalayas happened when the plate carrying India pushed into the plate carrying Asia. This crushing has been going on for 100 million years and it is still continuing.

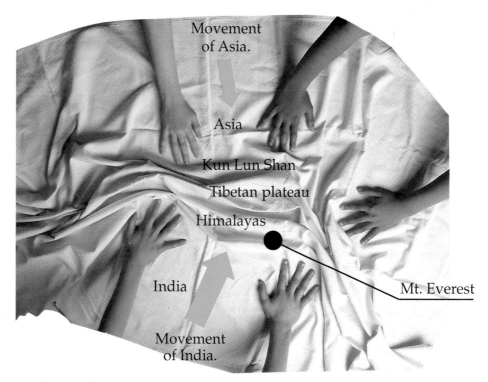

This table cover model shows the broad pattern of folded ranges in the Himalayas made using the technique shown on page 21. To get accurate information on ranges you should refer to an atlas.

New words

block mountain
a mountain formed when a large block of crust is pushed up or when surrounding blocks move down. The block mountain is surrounded by shear sides made by repeated faulting

cirque
a bowl-shaped hollow eroded into a mountain by ice. In places where cirques have melted away, the hollow often fills with water to make a circular lake

crust
the name for the upper part of the Earth, usually the top 10 to 100 mi. The rocks of the crust are hard and cold. Below lie the molten hot rocks of the region called the mantle

earthquake
the name given to violent ground shaking. It is caused by rocks moving past each other along a fault. The strength of earthquakes is measured on a scale called the Richter scale

erosion
the removal of rock and soil from the land by rivers, wind and ice

erupt
the outpouring of molten material, either lava or ash, from a volcano during one of its active periods. Eruptions usually only last between a few days and a few months

fault
a break in the rocks of the crust. Faults sometimes cause land to be lifted into mountain ranges

fold mountain
a mountain which has been formed as two of the Earth's plates move together, crumpling up the rocks in between

lava
the molten material that flows from an active volcano during an eruption. Lava is red or orange in color when it erupts, but soon cools to a black rock often full of trapped bubbles

mountain chain
a series of mountain ranges stretching thousands of miles across a continent

mountain range
a single narrow ridge of mountains separated from other ranges by valleys

plate
a large piece of the crust of the Earth that is split away from the other parts of the crust and which can move slowly over the Earth's surface, driven by forces deep within the Earth

scree
broken rock that has fallen from a mountain and which builds up into a fan-shape in the valley below

U-shaped valley
the deep trench cut by a glacier as it flows from a mountain

volcano
a place where lava and ash are erupting at the Earth's surface. Lava and ash usually build up around the eruption, making a cone-shaped mountain

Index